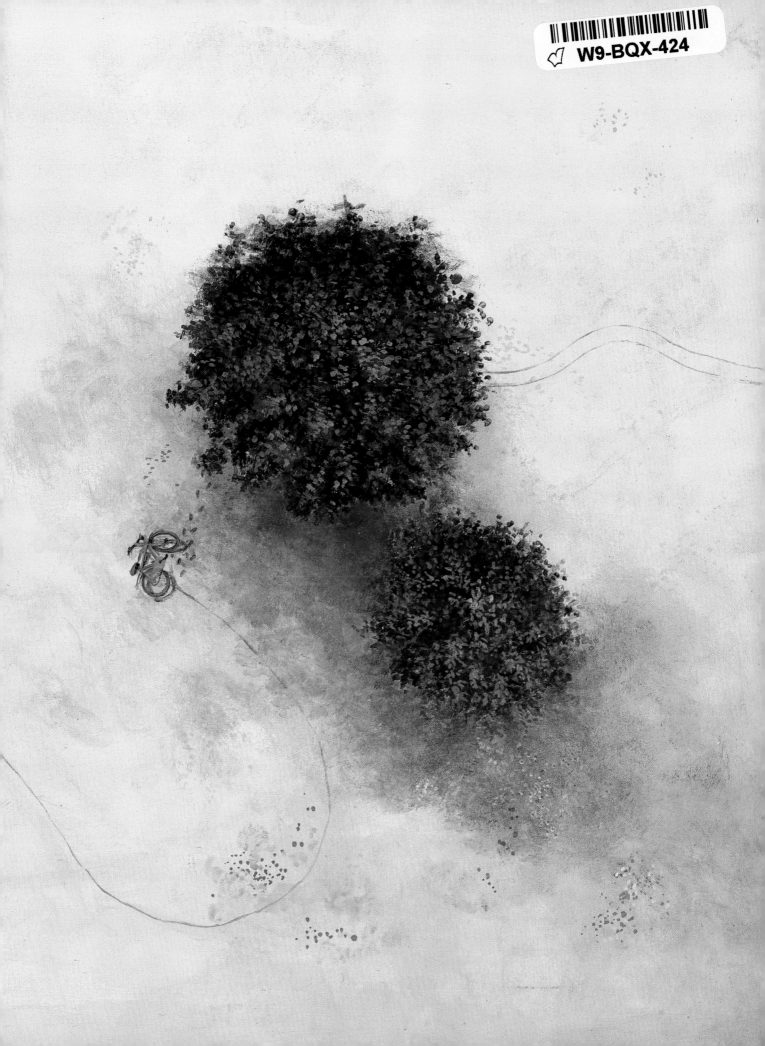

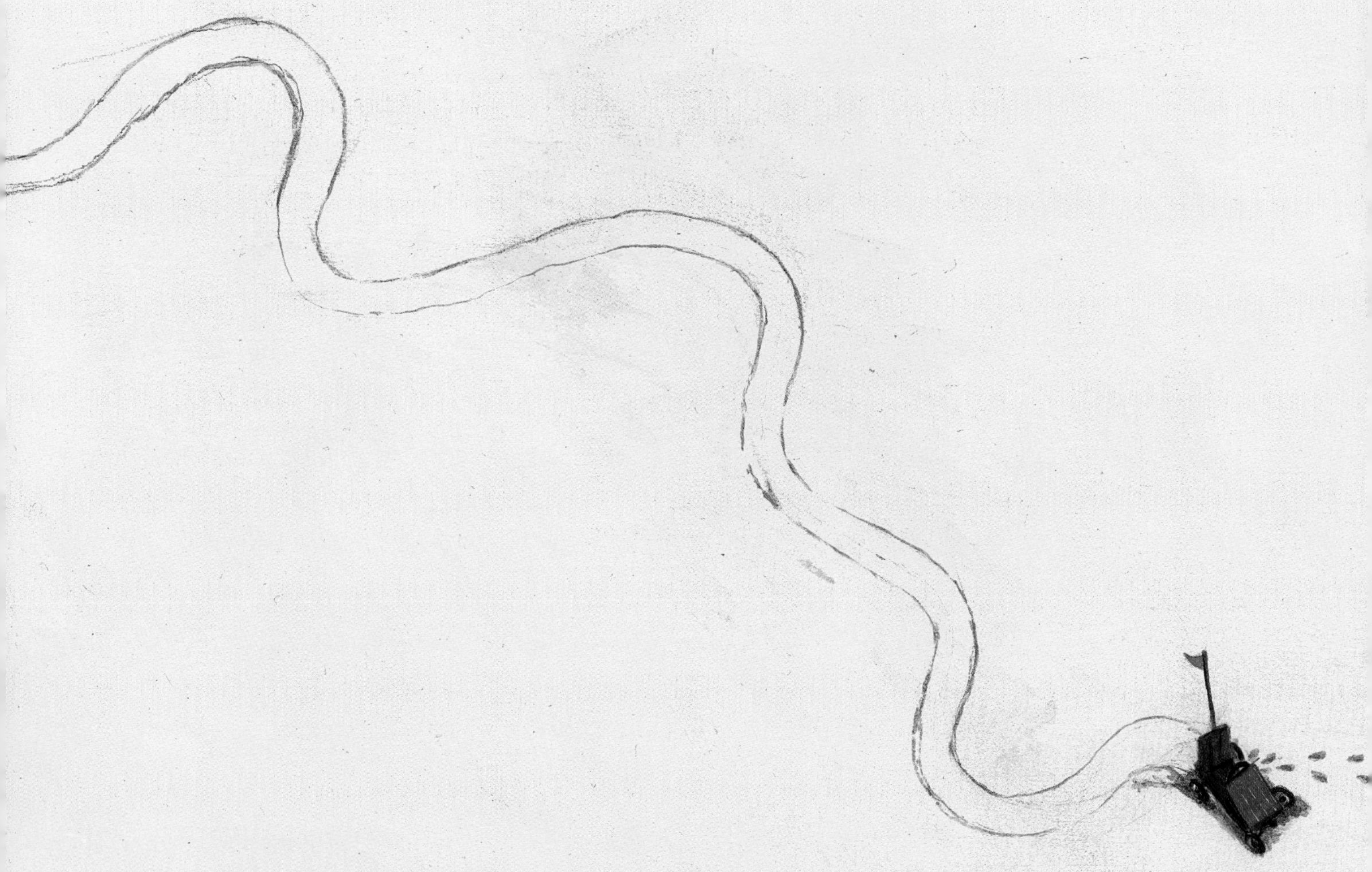

ISBN 1-886910-65-0

Printed and bound in Belgium
First American edition

Let's Go

Charlotte Dematons

Front Street Lemniscaat

Come on!

Let's go to the store for some apples.

I'm wearing a red shirt.

Follow me!

Let's *run* through the forest.

There might be dragons.

There could be a giant sleeping in the dark.

Walk softly so he doesn't wake up.

Let's climb over the rocks.

Look! A boat!

Hop in. Quick!

We'll row out to sea.

Wow!

I sure hope there aren't any whales out here.

Row fast! There are pirates on that boat.

Where are we?

Come on. Follow me!

Over here. Let's hide in this bush.

We can sneak past the pirates' den.

We made it! But where were we going?

Oh right. To buy apples.

How do we get back?

Maybe we should just take the sidewalk?

Dematons, Charlotte.

Let's go.

$15.95

DATE			

BAKER & TAYLOR